To Jan and Wiebke

—Heather

❧

To the loudest herd I know-Gabriel,
Merci Maguire, Maeve, and Guinevere

—Eileen

Sleeping Bear Press™

2395 South Huron Parkway, Suite 200, Ann Arbor, MI 48104
www.sleepingbearpress.com
© Sleeping Bear Press

Printed and bound in the United States.
10 9 8 7 6 5 4 3 2 1

Library of Congress Cataloging-in-Publication Data

Names: Preusser, Heather, 1977- author. | Ewen, Eileen Ryan, illustrator.
Title: A symphony of cowbells / by Heather Preusser ; [illustrated by] Eileen Ryan Ewen.
Description: Ann Arbor, MI : Sleeping Bear Press, [2017] | Summary: "Each
spring Petra and her family lead their cows into the pastures and each cow
wears her own jangling bell. When Petra's favorite cow loses her bell
the whole herd is out of harmony and refuses to move. Will Petra be able
to find Elfi's bell before it's too late?" Provided by the publisher.
Identifiers: LCCN 2016030977 | ISBN 9781585369683
Subjects: | CYAC: Cows–Fiction. | Cowbells–Fiction. | Lost and found possessions–Fiction.
Classification: LCC PZ7.1.P75 Sy 2017 | DDC [E]–dc23
LC record available at https://lccn.loc.gov/2016030977

A Symphony of Cowbells

Heather Preusser and Eileen Ryan Ewen

Spring in Gimmelwald
was the **loudest** season.

Da-ding, da-ding.

Jingle-jangle, jingle-jangle.

Clang-clong-clank, clang-clong-clank.

With the warmer weather, the family's dairy cows paraded to the high meadows, where the grass was greenest. Their sweet milk was turned into scrumptious cheese and sold by the wedge, wheel, and wagonload. During the trek, each cow wore her own clanging bell. Petra's favorite cow, Elfi, wore the most booming brass bell of all.

Brrring-BONG, brrring-BONG.

But one morning, when Petra joined the herd in the lower meadows, she noticed Elfi's familiar melody was missing.

"Where's your bell, sweet girl?" asked Petra.

Elfi hung her head.

"She'll have to make do without one," said Petra's father.
"We have a schedule to keep."

Elfi stamped her hoof.

"Let's go, Elfi," Petra said, pulling.
"Let's go, Elfi," Petra's father said, pushing.
They pulled and they pushed
until they dug themselves into a rut.

Da-ding, da-ding.

Jingle-jangle, jingle-jangle.

Clang-clong-clank, clang-clong-clank.

"MooooOOOOOooooo," said Elfi.

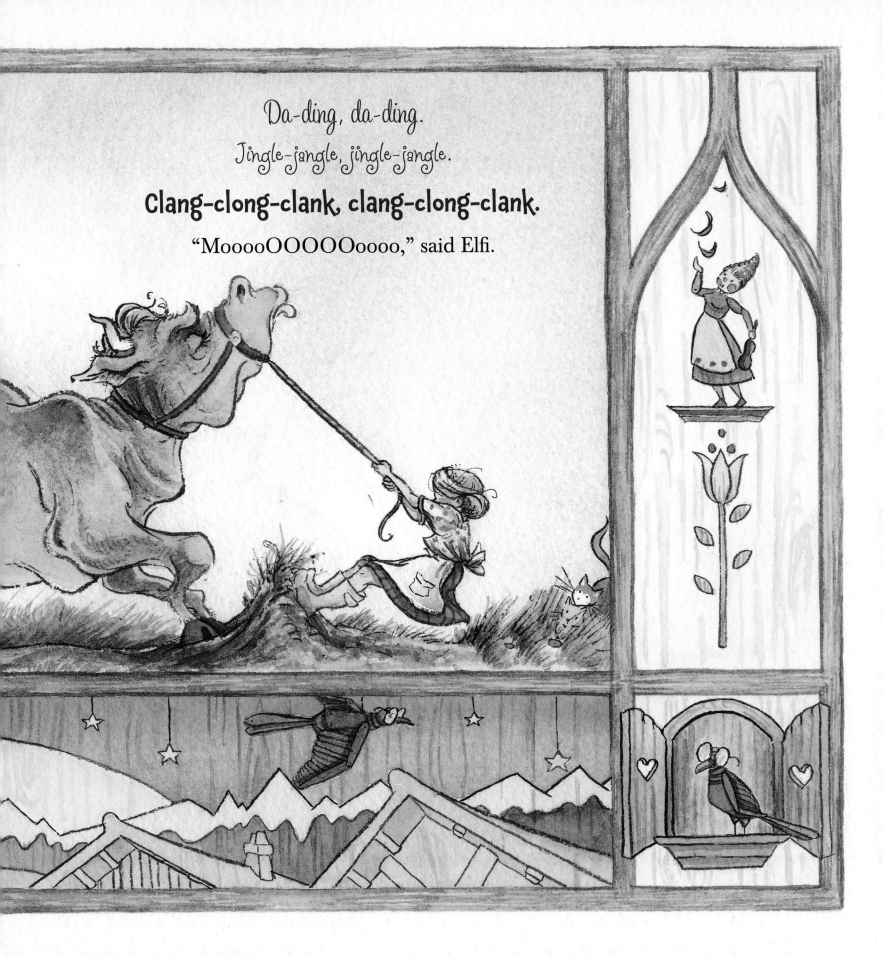

"How about a different bell, Elfi?"
asked Petra, hanging a tiny tin bell
on the caramel-colored cow.

Elfi sniffed and snorted at the embarrassing tinkling.

Tittle-tattle-tink, tittle-tattle-tink.

The other cows gawked at Elfi.

Tittle-tattle-tink, tittle-tattle-tink.

"Something is out of tune,"
said Petra's father. And one by one,
the stubborn cows lay down.

"The herd won't move unless
it's in perfect harmony!"
Tittle-tattle-tink, tittle-tattle-tink.
"No milk? No cheese? What'll we do?"
Petra gulped. She looked at Elfi,
her eyes wide as milk saucers.
"Elfi, please MOOOVE!"

"MooooOOOOOoooo," said Elfi.

"We must find that brass bell!" said Petra.

They searched around the house . . .
. . . in the barn . . .
. . . and through the field.
No bell.

The stubborn cows remained rooted among the bellflowers.
Night fell and silence rang throughout the valley.

The next morning, while picking a bouquet
full of sweet, tasty flowers for Elfi, Petra
spotted a crow carrying something shiny.
Petra followed the bird past the meadow,
where neighbors were cutting hay . . .

. . . past the house, where Petra's parents
were doing morning chores . . .

. . . to a large nest.

Petra stood on her tippy-toes, but the nest was much too high.

The neighbors balanced on each other.
Petra's father balanced on the neighbors.
Petra's mother balanced on Petra's father.
And Petra balanced on her mother.

Petra reached up the rock face, into the nest,
and found Mr. Schmid's pocket watch,
Miss Baumann's reading glasses,
Farmer Felber's wrench, Mother's bracelet,
Father's keys, and . . . Elfi's brass bell!
Petra swung it back and forth. It made a magnificent melody.

Brrring-BONG, brrring-BONG.

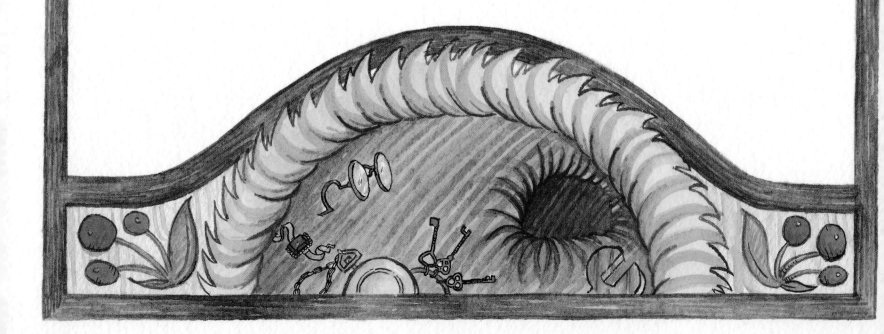

Petra clambered down from the nest.

She dashed past the house . . .

Brrring-BONG, brrring-BONG.

. . . past the meadow . . .

Brrring-BONG, brrring-BONG.

. . . and up to her four-legged friend.
Brrring-BONG, brrring-BONG.

Elfi pranced in circles. "MooooOOOOOoooo!"
She recognized her bell instantly.

Petra kissed Elfi's nose.

Elfi nuzzled Petra's cheek as the girl traded the tiny tin bell
for the big brass bell, the **tittle-tattle-tink** for the **brrring-BONG.**

The other cows turned their heads and twitched their tails.
On cue, they stood and moseyed up the mountainside.

Brrring-BONG, brrring-BONG. *Da-ding, da-ding.*

Elfi held her head high. The symphony of cowbells
was harmonious again—and LOUD.
It was spring in Gimmelwald after all.

Jingle-jangle, jingle-jangle.

Clang-clong-clank, clang-clong-clank.